Tibi vero gratias agam quo clamore?

—ATHANASIUS KIRCHER

In his *Annunciation,* Simone Martini paints the Virgin's *small mouth turned down/Her thumb holding a book open*—startled to be interrupted, or preserving her story before the story about to begin. In *Clamor,* her third collection, Ann Lauterbach elicits the radical disturbances of narrative, the lacunae between the event and its depiction, between seeing and saying, *looking at and being in.* Collapsing such dualities, she explores the ways in which language voices desire—the world named and present in its images—and loss—the world recalled, or absent, in its telling.

The self wonders and wanders among these gaps, myriad as a clamorous crowd or solitary as an amorous lover awaiting an embrace, not a static and coherent entity, but an agent and aspect of response. Often, the fleeting image of a girl—holding the book open; *tethered to a small town as to a door held open;* undressing; spilling the wine; *separating figure from ground and solving it*—moves through the poems, seeking *to know what nobody else ever knew.*

It is in the permutating web of language, Lauterbach tells us, in the elisions between world and word, chance and change, that our human potential inheres. This she shows with the wit, eloquence, and exuberance of the seventeenth-century Jesuit Kircher's urgent declension: *amore, more, ore, re* (with thy love, thy wont, thy words, thy deeds). *What time is it?* the poet asks. Time to wake up, *because because* and *now now now.*

THE PENGUIN POETS

CLAMOR

Ann Lauterbach was born and grew up in Manhattan, where she attended the High School of Music and Art. A graduate of the University of Wisconsin at Madison, she spent seven years in London, where she worked as an editor, teacher, and as director of the literature program at the Institute of Contemporary Arts. Since returning to New York, she has worked in a number of art galleries, written art criticism, and taught in the writing programs at Columbia, Princeton, and Iowa. She now is a professor at The City College of New York. She is the recipient of a Guggenheim Fellowship, as well as grants from the New York Council for the Arts and the Ingram Merrill Foundation. She has been, since 1981, a contributing editor of *Conjunctions* magazine.

ANN LAUTERBACH

Penguin Books

CLAMOR

PENGUIN BOOKS
Published by the Penguin Group
Viking Penguin, a division of Penguin Books USA Inc.,
375 Hudson Street, New York, New York 10014, U.S.A.
Penguin Books Ltd, 27 Wrights Lane, London W8 5TZ, England
Penguin Books Australia Ltd, Ringwood, Victoria, Australia
Penguin Books Canada Ltd, 2801 John Street, Markham, Ontario, Canada L3R 1B4
Penguin Books (N.Z.) Ltd, 182–190 Wairau Road, Auckland 10, New Zealand

Penguin Books Ltd, Registered Offices:
Harmondsworth, Middlesex, England

First published in the United States of America by Viking Penguin,
a division of Penguin Books USA Inc. 1991
Published in Penguin Books 1992

1   3   5   7   9   10   8   6   4   2

Acknowledgment is made to the following publications, in which some of the poems
in this book appeared originally: *American Poetry Review*: "Untoward," "Santa Fe Sky,"
"Tuscan Visit (Simone Martini)," "Gesture and Flight," "Blue Iris," "Notes from a
Conversation," "Broken Skylight"; *The Antioch Review*: "Tribe (Stamina of the Unseen),"
"Clamor," "Annotation," "Further Thematics"; *Broadway 2*: "Day"; *Columbia: A Mag-
azine of Poetry and Prose*: "Report"; *Conjunctions*: "Mountain Roads," "Tock," "Revenant,"
"After the Storm," "Of the Meadow," "The French Girl," "How Things Bear Their
Telling," "Prom in Toledo Night"; *New American Writing*: "Lakeview Diner," "Local
Branch," "Werner Herzog 68/Iowa City 88," "Night Rehearsal"; *o·blēk*: "The Elaborate
Absence"; *Pequod*: "Boy Sleeping"; *Quarterly West*: "A Documentary."

"How Things Bear Their Telling" was published separately by Collectif Generation,
Colombes, France, with drawings by Lucio Pozzi.

LIBRARY OF CONGRESS CATALOGING IN PUBLICATION DATA
Lauterbach, Ann, 1942–
Clamor/Ann Lauterbach.
p.   cm.
ISBN 0-14-058673-3
I. Title.
[PS3562.A844C57   1991]
811'.54—dc20   91-3873

Printed in the United States of America
Set in Garamond No. 3
Designed by Kate Nichols

To the memory of my sister Jennifer

and for her sons

John Lloyd Robbins

Richard Edward Robbins

There I cannot find There
I cannot hear your wandering prayer
of quiet

—SUSAN HOWE

So silence is pictorial
when silence is real.

—BARBARA GUEST

The author wishes to thank the following persons for their assistance, guidance, and good cheer: Paul Auster, Jena Osman, Edward Barrett, Arthur Vogelsang, and Bradford Morrow. A special thanks to Nan Graham for all those things and more.

To the Ingram Merrill Foundation, The New York Foundation for the Arts and, somewhat belatedly, to The Guggenheim Foundation, my gratitude for their support.

CONTENTS

III. THE ELABORATE ABSENCE

I

REMORSE OF THE DEPICTED

MOUNTAIN ROADS

I.

There is this chronic scouting, as from
Under the humid pose of these days,
Scouting the city, not as mild tourists
Lifting their bare arms from street to street
Acquiring, but as ourselves,
Not quite exhausted,
Neither surprised nor pleased to find
Trompe l'oeil windows peeling off brick
As our journey continues, endlessly awkward.
You know what I mean? I mean the desire
To crouch and loosen earth, toss pebbles,
Pull the taut grass at its roots
And wonder what to do with a fat rope of old vine.
Or maybe something so intimate
We are seared and tame, brought into focus
By only one image: clear fluid among weeds;
A clear drop of fluid resting at the tip of a stamen.
The old problem surfaces into the longest twilight.
What time is it? A lance of rosemary,
A ballad, and the hermit thrush
Appeal to us directly, distract us from it.
It we say often, and it is always the same it.
In the magazine of our choice, it is our theme,
Almost a mirror held up to our face, my face, then, mine
Remarking. O but that girl's loveliness is the same
As the path's: surprise and loveliness there
Where wild, surprising fragrances at last delay our pursuit.

II.

The great rims, upwardly dark and darkly elongated,
Are boundaries we must, like it or not, accept.
I wonder where the trails were?
We are this much emptied, as if no news
Or no news yet, and we know what can no longer be
Assured. We were progressive
And we were cosmetic; briefly, we were in the grips
Of awe, like the mild tourists pointing
And the girl smiling down into the pond.
She has not yet seen her face, she has seen
Only the Greek poet searching a soul for his soul.
But she has been riding the shaped water in a small boat,
Scanning for admissable events. It is twilight and,
From the edge of the wood, a hermit thrush
Begins to memorize the tentative
And to seduce us directly.
Pretty soon we'll start remembering
All over again, but there were no weddings.
There were no weddings that June. Instead,
Numbers of us left for Maine and Italy.
Maine was an old standby, a place
Where you could paint the air.
Italy? The land there tilts
So that you are forced to look up
Searching the skies for something beyond nature
But still contained by it. It was, as I recall,
A summer decisive for its impact.
Everything tasted fresh and nothing much was sacrificed.

LAKEVIEW DINER

for Jack

A chair, half-hidden behind leaves;
A torso, emerging from pigment;
A girl, on the outskirts;
This is how all my beginnings are.
I fell asleep reading a book.
Was the brief dream astute?
We know memory is crooked, is interlude,
But natural elision is part of our booty,
And is why I cannot know myself
Better than you do, and you know me
Better than I. I resemble the girl
In the paragraph. So here we are,
Each of us, in the abrasive gleam
Of our settings, hunched over sections
Of the newspaper. We greet each other
With the unobtrusive fanfare of a waitress:
"Howdy folks, what'll it be today?"
Her hand on a rag. Her hand on the rag
Steers from edge to edge, like a wind
Over the lake. "I'd like
The late afternoon reflected in the lake
And that upturned leaf which appears to be a duck.
Hold the light." This is how all my middles are.
Now we can relax against the speaking other,
Like the adjacent dawn leaning on its day,
Furthering. But what? The trap and scandal
We voted for yesterday, but did not choose.
Know ye what ye want, said the wise man,
But be sure ye knoweth the consequences
Of what ye want. So now we embark
On the chill voyage out into the numbered
Scheme of things.

And the days swarm up and away
Into the agility of brief reverence;
The duck returns to a leaf.
Call these actions ourselves delayed.
We are kept by the indefinite, aroused.

LOCAL BRANCH

for Stacy Doris

The chill impediments—caution, doubt,
Yoking us again to the clandestine trap

Where wonder, like a strange forgiveness,
Comes in from the hollow

Whose word I had recently
Held or clasped, had altered, refused

Finally in this round of seeing's belief,
The mind watching itself depart

As the girl I now own, her
Pattern of rushing away to escape

That other, less mild convergence
As to a page, a mast, another's insistence.

The warranted came stressed, adoptive,
Who was that masked man but an idea

Of the eternal, fictive and obscene,
Forever transcribed but broken, incoherent.

I told her, but first I asked her
To tell me and she told me: this, if not

Another, would be this.
Seems plausible, if abhorrent, and so

Wisdom came to play against the backdrop.
How does it look? Like a broken—

Like wandering from the story, telling it
Backwards, telling it in an irretrievable code.

Then this light flipped in the rowboats
Then this anchor lifted from petulant water
Like a stem. Neither chimes nor chills nor vanes,
Wheels wheeling, deadpan, the young man
Had taken his crew so far to this island,
This wind, to find them and, eventually,
To take us there.
                It was a small city
It was
      the light released, skyward, not
Natural and I wondered how many of them
Were dead having gone from the frame.
                  It was
Like a wedding of strangers previously arranged,
The bride in her gown of fetid rosebuds
Forgetting her lines, smiling
Despite the feet in the wall,
Despite the illusion.
          It was
Another film in the small city where a man
Saw the most beautiful woman ever
In the ugliest hat.
         It was a hen trapped in sand.
It was, finally, a young boy not knowing what to say
Now that he was able to say it, a young girl
Singing, twisting up her skirt, her mouth dark.
It was a war nobody had ever heard of, a child
Touching the sleeve of a stranger.

FORGETTING THE LAKE

Look, this leaving may last indefinitely
Branching into the cool siphons
Of this first last afternoon which is filling
Or spilling an atmosphere of sensuality.
I am hoping to go on with or in it
Aided only by the redundant silence
We have come to expect from these moods
With their pleasurable anxieties
Calling from the fringes and shores—
Latent words or dreams coming up shortly
In the new night. There are holes in the fabric
And holes in the ground where light and roots are
Taking hold in usual ways, plantings and reflections
Too numerous to name but worth noticing
As holding actions against the next, less generous phase.
What I want to do is say
What will not be mistaken and will withstand
The assorted claims on our attention, and I mean our,
Yours, and mine. The vases are finished, perhaps forever,
They are dimming with wildflowers that will not last either.

Everything I am thinking of rhymes with *spires*
So this could turn into a game
In which you are temporarily lost
In our common forest, and begin to turn slowly
And to look up to see where the sun is.
The sun is a clue, as in *fires, expires*
But I could help you back to the path
With my staff, my handwrought cane, my smile
That tells you not to be afraid I know the way by heart.
. . .

The formula for forgetting is different
From city to city, city to country: each
Has its own tradition of gazing,
Its indigenous wings to intercept and shadow
The critiques that ensue, late-breaking
Like the news, but never on the news.
This is the jazz hour, the hour of recent releases,
Which used to be the cocktail hour in Easthampton.
Does each act of forgetting allow for new memory,
Is this part of the economy?
The dark is still coming; the wind has picked up.
But who will remember?
The dark is still coming; the wind has picked up.
I have doubled the possibility
But duplications are endless: each day has its own.
Are you still lost in the woods? The clouds
Will never part and I am already home, baking
Blueberry muffins, listening to jazz, lights on.

UNTOWARD

Reading, I spilled the wine.
Do you care? Are you wet? Do you care?
In a later epistle, hands dry, I will say
What is not so, although
Something may come of it.
The instance, allowed to speak, is not yet
Embodied, the big vacancies filled with bigness
As from beyond, or behind, an image:
A serpent hides in a tree,
A man falls into an abyss.
I spilled the wine or the wine escaped.
A gaze enhances the partial stain.
He might have drowned in the eclipsed target
Its drum first inscribed and wiped clean
Before I arrived. What day? What month?
Was it here, enduring the long facade of evening
Like a favorite monk extolling his service.
Omit distance; forbid silence.
Gain a dry incentive's leap.
I spilled the wine: eyes dry, hands wet.
And whatever new choice, whatever limit.

He stood up as if to wander.
Cloudy again, distributed thinly, unanimous.
Are you wondering? Are you clear?
The decision omitted its conclusion, obviously:
I crossed only to here, another invitation
Without fruition, and no need for boots, gloves, hat.
When asked if I had written about her
I said no, not exactly. She became the wild.

MEANWHILE THE TURTLE

for Gloria Jacobs

(Not even the lame grass can answer this *what is this*
Thread of body, injunction to seem,
The ricochet robot blurting its mind
In these aftermaths & retreats, as if singing.
Say you heard it all before in the crisp dawn.
Say you were held delighted in duration:
The giddy kingfisher's clack and surround
Above water while the mower rackets air.
Shorn, divested, complicit asunder or sender
Forthwith enjambed in the yellow sound of yellow.
Maybe someone else was talking in the next room.
Maybe the big man lay with a spoon in his mouth
Lest he swallow his tongue, or was coiled
Sleeping in the stairwell while someone's mother wept.
We had nameless signs we could read.
Nobody told me to confess.
There was an old fear, hearing the planes,
Believing our anthem's threat: the noise is real.
Anyone can see there are gaps in the leaves.
Anyone can tell the sky is in disrepair.
But also an accumulation, being wounded
Similarly with just the wind to embrace
In the pallid sky's stormy indoctrination.
Not just any shard underfoot, but a long nail
Up through the heel, a child's wrist broken) is lost.

A DOCUMENTARY

Time being what it is,
Prophetic and absent while we are here
Suspended in the good distance,
Each a figure in a composition we later desire,
It seems to ask us to declare ourselves
As more than witness, to be its bearing on us.
And that is what we are
When our sayings float back
Like the shadow of loose kites
Rising over the field, reminding us
Of an event that has perished
And goes on perishing while we build
Against the foraging wind, whose agent
Is disguised in our folly, its indifference
Flapping down on our habits
The way the long-beaked stork flaps onto nests
And tweezes out fledglings.
This is when haunting comes
And this is when we hide,
Closing the hall door against the irreparable damage
In the kitchen, and against the countertenor's voice
Which seeps in anyway, makes its way
To where we are about to sleep
So we must move on, set out to find
What we thought we saw in the sailor's eyes
When he told of his days at sea.

TOCK

A night without edition, virtual:
A hearing. Yes, and yes its sleeve
Gapes to house the air's thin shine.
An old path is traced
Obscurely along the meridian
Near to where our ancient kin were
And were buried in loam, preserving them.
A smooth crest, a young boy's brow.
I walked with him one afternoon in winter
As the ferns shook under the dazzling rise.

Under the dazzling rise the ferns shake
Verdigris on copper. This day
We go to the field where a battle was lost.
We see them toppled on the plain
Like ropes frayed, untwisted.
He says, *I am going to kiss you here.*
We meet barefoot girls
Weeping, their footsteps in damp, torn grass.
In damp grass, tearing air, the girls weep.

The women are sad, and old.
They picket the house.
Now the girls are in a barn
Where they will be photographed by men
Who smell of oil and straw and brandy.
The walls are hung with useful tools, straps.
Later, the barn is a staircase
Hung with pictures of children smiling.
They are on a ladder. The roofline extends.
The roofline is an arm extending the night.

REVENANT

The world had sallied forth, unmeasured.
I heard it. I heard it as *branch*.
And I saw your eyes climb
Into their passages, little bony cups
Worn against the newest weather
Its eloquence forced upon us
As frugal, unspeakable knowledge.
A shiver of false fire
Warmed us stupidly, and the needles lay about
On the floor and on the pillows.
Your name was like something laid
There also against diminishment
And I said it to tear the firmament freshly
When words turn against their truths
Like traitors. Gaze and know my face,
Come back to the sunshine now rambling
Over the occasion like a mute apology,
Asking forgiveness for accepting the part
In the first place. We are near each other
In the gathered promise of a girl
Who remembers the city as a transparent bridle,
Her long hand reaching out of danger to find refuge.

AFTER THE STORM

What the afternoon assumes is
That we will live through it, as well as in it.
But what if, in thunder, in high wet wind,
It tore from us, left us here
Unframed in the raw conduit, marginal
And scared? Were it truly haphazard
It would be like that
But we must trust, we must be game.

I will tell you about the soprano
And I will tell you about the cool air's form.
Writing now, I think of her,
Of how she smiles into the capitulated yes
Of her ruined kindness, her voice
Swaddled in archives of her self.
She sings into the butterfly weed and fog
Only it is not a song, it is

Her desire to sing and her desire not to sing.
The wet, heavy fog rolls in
And the weed is burning at the edge of the meadow.
Her trouble is the trouble of fiction and dolls;
She is authored by another, one who says
Sing! Do not sing! and does not watch
As the weed fires along the meadow
And does not see the fog roll over her toward us.

REPORT

Too much drudgery binds the tongue.
The obdurate loosens its hold,
A nonchalant mask foiling
A reward as of a natural sling
Garlanded, sleepless, fervent.
It had asked us to come away
And to touch everything we passed
Down the staircase hollow,
Under the blue rocks,
Into the broken bodies distributed
Where alms could not reach,
Between the curtains and the glass,
On the stinking sheets,
Into the smoke-scented air's pulleys,
The inexhaustible list of lists
And its absurd author's abject test.
Why did I come inside to tell you this?
Did someone call? Do I remember being called?
To wash, yes, to eat, yes, to sleep
But not to step over the shape
Curled in the hall, its body's huge loop
Hung in the mind like a shadow
That must be surpassed. Had I been asked
To tidy the forest floor, *pick it up, pick it up,*
Dead boughs, tiny gray leaves, stone upon stone,
Dust, wings, moss, and fill up the holes
Of each sarcophagus leeching icy water,
Mend the ripped ferns, untie the knots
Of each web and nest. Had I said
No I will follow this trail, these subjects
Until they are depleted
Because all the women and girls came in.

REMORSE OF THE DEPICTED

for Chet Wiener

Harsh brag of the inexhaustible: *replete, replete.*
Lured away from choice as from extreme devotion.
Another time, friendships will soften
Into broader categories, letting gaps heal.
The undoing that ending is
Is prettier if less abrasive
So we might come and go in aspects:
I'll keep his face, her hands, your voice
Observing the necessary between.
Words cling to other words
As we have seen, although even these are
Migratory and the forgotten shows through as correction.
This noun has been defunct for centuries.
May I have it, just this once, this while
Upon which the wind is so insistent?
Collage has made a chaos of my desk.
But the interior strain is intolerable
When character is evoked: under the ashtray,
A young girl's eyes looking out from her image.
Was she brave? Have I told you about my uncle,
My cousin, my mother seeing a tall man on some steps
And deciding there and then on my life?
In your dream, you were flayed
By the inflection of recovered speech, the earlier
Moment in a dark car with an old friend driving.
Things we don't do take up residence as facts
And, as facts, we desire them. I wonder how my garden is.

DAY

A broken candor's unruly sham
And the blue dawn's blinking blue

The innumerable cause of the just begun
And the body's willing hemispheres

Revising inaccurately taut
Always an impossible clause

As an echo trapped in a pond
And green frozen feathers

Waiting to be upon
Waiting to be open

The sky I say is an adulating glass
Neither empty nor hollow, inhumanly full

About to be done
And the lunar paste

Episodic   convivial   receptive
Who could say what would be said

After the mobile *as if*
Swayed and plunged, skittering on ice

A dry incentive
Wisp of hard hair

No ballast in the rare wind's
Fleet indoctrination

. . .

Sockets of the newly dead
Individual tangles of broken pipe

And the same illusory blue
Is the sack of another day

Triumphant
Whose finite gaze

Shifting
Her self almost gone

Into the private sector
Where each of us will be

But for the cast and carriage
Each revision is.

SANTA FE SKY

A spare radiance blooms, blooms again, expires.
This is the radical mark
Of an insatiable wish.
Things look like other things, as was said.
Those that are unleashed
Come upon the hot earth
Toward the toward, violently
Unproven. Thrall is a curse,
A woven rival place indissolubly conditioned.
This you may have seen and endured
As it came nearer, threading its term.
But to act would be the vanishing we know:
Ocean in its wholeness, river in its time,
Lake holding the persistent, domestic sky,
Each an episode in the will to be parted.
But to be that, to be weather
In the distance, fallen, dreamed of; also imagined.

II
TRIBE
(STAMINA OF THE
UNSEEN)

OF THE MEADOW

1.

Did you like Switzerland? you ask for the first time
And motion for someone else to take the wheel.
Trope of what? You are no one's mother,
No one's daughter-in-law,
And are not exemplary.
                              What of the meadow?
Lavish, syntactic, new in the natural key
But frugal and obscure in translation.
So you want to put it in a jar
On the mantelpiece to steer us in a direction,
Into casual excellence, once wild.
Something about it makes you hurry
Before the next one comes along
To render it formal, instructive, true.
You want to be known
As the one who got out from under,
Who survived the winter. But
Yesterday I heard you say *shredded, dice,*
Taking what you could get, like a stranger.

2.

Say, *We did not get what we came for*
And proceed to your destination
Like a commercial without sound.
You strip away the drama's script
And come to the task refreshed.
Days pass, with rain, with mice
Busy in the eaves; another pond nearby.
Engage it to drain or flush

The episode out: kneeling, as children,
Against the event, plucking a bloom
From the Chinese screen which, you believe,
Later went up in flames. But that could be
Only the fatigue of memory washed clean,
Bleached, newly ransacked and incredulous
But for its renown, wandering
The upper tier of a proscenium
Garbed in quotations, acquisitions,
Sheets of white linen already, initially, inscribed.
You tell yourself to wait, say
The actor is the audience, the audience asleep
On a bench in a park in a small city
That the troupe might visit.
The water seems to lengthen in the breeze.
Later, you dream the image, adding time to space,
And someone, correctly, says, *We knew all along
That the city was beautiful.* So things
Manage to go on in a parade of similarities:
Lilies on this pond, that pond.
And the long curtains divide
Still touching the shore, the stage, the glass.

3.

On the pier, among the banished,
Sealed away from the hot toys
Listed on the page as *fable*
Our sightseeing continues
Like a flock risen from ashes
Where the fire stood bequeathed, or stolen.
Where are the matches? I had asked, my feet

Wet from long grass.
That girl keeps running by the door.
That man keeps asking questions.
You keep saying, in answer to mine,
No, I am happy.
                    So I go on coming to it
As to the edge of water,
Blind with a fiction of recovery.
Is this what you meant by persistence?
The voice recorded into mimicry,
The water folding light into its surface,
The girl materializing like a path along the ridge.
What are the signs, now
That you cannot correct the impression
As I arrange the flowers, as I notice the incomplete.

THE FRENCH GIRL

1.

Someone plays
              & the breaking mounts.
Raw material for worthy forthcoming;
Indecipherable, discrete.
                   Plays
Rhapsodies as the air cools
And vanquishes: nothing sits still, yet.
The land is a result of its use, I explained.
Everything else rested while the kids made a girdle
Removed from classical syntax. Shed, and

Something breaks, mounting
The small hill to its vista: I saw
A rope of trees in another country.
I could not say *I am lost* in the proper way.
The season is huge.
This house is haunted: I planted it.
Where? In the shed, and

Spoiled by attention. You see?
Every bit counts, when the morning displays
The serious ratio of the given stars.
What made us tear the hours into lines?
So things became a burden to shed, and

Astute as a hungry pilgrim
But not brave, sucking and expert.
It is impolite to stare. Is unwise
To plunder the easily forgotten,
Easily shed, and

2.

They drummed and drummed, attached to a vestigial
Clamor. The heat splayed; sparklers
Ravished the fog.
Morning tore the dead back to shore;
Enemy ships floundered and were forgotten.
Still, nothing was appeased:
The living silhouette drifted into view
Like an ephemeral sail promoting ease
Between wreckages.
                              Not speaking a word of English
She animated the landscape
With abundance, a chosen self
Freely translated into the color of her eyes.
Awkward and luminous, a stilted charm
Separating figure from ground, and solving it.
What pushed us toward the abysmal
With such new appraisals, such sure interest?
The mute girl had seen glories
But what had she come to know?
A finite figure in a rainy field.
A naked figure in a pool.
A skipping figure across a bridge.
A lost figure on a city street.
A moaning figure on a huge bed.
A smiling face in a photograph.
All summer, I circled the garden for her sake.

TRIBE (STAMINA OF THE UNSEEN)

1.

What estranged methods, what original repose.
The entailing ground, flat and firm enough,
Is littered and agreeable—to which, to which
Our own selves trail, hauling.
The wild cannot call.
Things are covered with paisley and stain.
Estranged and original, the system of recovery
Is still unknown as what is perceived
Proceeds to the near at hand.
                                    A stage, an address.
A willingness to submit to an interview: like to unlike.
Were we to permit this, were I to permit us,
The room would sail into open domain: there
Where the farms have settled.
Hauling, as from elsewhere,
And crafted now into mild or bitter climates,
Their shapes loaded into the sentence, molten,
Resembling maps. As each ends, another gains its forebears,
Angling into the emulsion as a need to be present.
The bride tries on a gown.
Rain lets fall its expedient veil
Listing its terms, less known, less coherent,
Than the troth of difference.

2.

Permitting us, I cannot tell how marvels are broken
Or what dispersals settled back into the common life.
Here the bitch comes in an aftermath of identity

Thinking herself memorable, having saved best for last.
That she is cold is irrefutable (the bride, the veil)
Eyes fledged from the immodest glare of regard,
Limbs accurately hungered. So we huddle
On the distressed, inarticulate streets
For as long as it takes
Before we lift from the denuded shelf
Its harvest.
                    Someone moans through thin walls
Between the sonata and football game, the new room
Fully achieved, listening for acquittal.
The blessing is ugly, unless you are there
For the final, blissful throb.
Tucked into the encounter
As the flip side of excess, boredom
Turns to passion, passion
To the closed glossary of events mimicked here.
A child might come along
Singing and radiant, sweetly adrift
On the wind's prow. She is a proposal.
She is uncensored, but for the conditions.
She quits the visible, a defiant intersection of modes,
Heaved, unstuck, estranged and original, saying
I am the issue. I am what you promised to do.

CLAMOR

1.

It was a trance: thieves, clowns, and the blind girl
Passed symmetrically under the wide structure
As a floor passes under a rug.
Was this enough to go on, this scrap?
Had I entered, or was I pacing the same limits:
The room brought forward to another landscape,
Its odd birds, its train, its street lamp
Stationed like an unmoving moon. At night, the cries
Assembled into the ordinary speech of lovers before love
As the train pulled up the space, passing and passing.
Were these categories to be kept—thief, clown, blind girl—
Or were they too narrowly forensic, too easily found,
The whining insatiable drift insufficiently modeled.
They were an invitation to appear, appease, applaud,
In short to respond, be magical.
In the old days, we howled.
In the old days we chanted our lists until they
Were deciphered, lifted the leaves, touched the broken clay,
Counted the steps quickly, saying this is the one with the key,
This is the one for whom I will awaken.

2.

Affection is merciless: the wind, the excluder.
So much ruptured attention, so much pillaged from the stalk.
Even the nerves stray from precision, announcing
Their stunned subject. Merciless: a field of snow
Flying like jargon, sweeping the issue away
In a halo of cold, its purpose
Lifted from the flat climate, from its nub or throb.

Lifted on impossible wings we are generous, we dare.
But affection is merciless: the dead in their thin garb
Walking the ruined streets, inventing us in stride and envy.
It is said they will make their way
Back to us, as what rises saves itself, falls.
What is the speed of this doctrine, what dividends,
What annual yield?
When will he give it back,
When will I laugh in the untidy yard
And when will her eyes, staring at me
Because she sees only her departure from me,
See me left here. Further adventure is further delay.
I used to count the days. I do not want to count the days.

ANNOTATION

Even accidents falter. The room behind the room
Has lost its particularity, a tent
In a field of tents.
These are like the endings of words
As rooms resemble the beginnings.
Will she choose? As between metal and cloth,
Duration over flexibility, easy handling, touch?
She lay in the brown October grass under an imported sky.
Or, standing inside, she gazes out at the real thing
Shifting behind glass.
To say sky in the face of sky
Is a failure of duration;
The sky escapes.
                 The suburbs are plain,
Especially in winter, if to be plain
Is to be similar. But this
Harbors difference in its midst.
Eventually it will become
The fabulous plaintiff absurdly jeweled,
A city ready to explore
All the oblique ruins of the unsaid.
The unhealed voices soar
Into the predawn like accelerating notes
In a choral mood. All night, she
Hears them, and turns away, and hears again
The refrain of the unspeakable rhyme
And wakes to first light spelling its shield.

FURTHER THEMATICS

An ear's tall cavern,
A mob climbing a twisted ladder with lunch pails,
A bowl of fruit in an unseen field,
Boys and girls lingering at the rails,
Elders in another language guarding the entrance,
Telling soldiers' lies, listening to the disordered music
Of the threshing floor.
These
Might heal the intemperate largesse.
These
Might enlarge the simple.

The resilience began to hurt.
Better to find names for the fallen,
For the reluctant and aggrieved
Missing from the precarious dissolves of the made,
Better to hunt in the marsh like a vagrant,
Call the dark-eyed boy
Beloved, his step quickening old words
In the nick of time, his hand mated to her back
As they uncoil the foreground, collapsing the known.
Her flames lick at the parchment path,
Her eyes lift, a plea
To watch as straw is flushed from the gutters,
The sleeping beasts toppled by wind,
The hugely girthed moon tossed
Up over the horizon.
Down by the river restaurant
The doctor is eating.
He eats there often, watching
The river snarl by the windows of the renovated factory:
Wood panels, flags woven by the lame, pipes

35

Painted and digestive mantling the walls.
The waiter is waxen with service.
Trained as an acrobat, he speaks fluent French,
Is writing a book about angels.
The salad bar attests to basic freedoms:
A choice of dressings; olives, chick-peas, carrots.
The doctor converses, listens to rumors,
A new law passed, a girl
Tethered to a small town as to a door held open,
Just as she was about to speak wisely and kindly
About the condition of women in her time.
She had begun, "You must attend to the surface
Stroke or touch, not just to the image, those blooms
Reduced to postcards or the flatness of calendars. . . ."
The doctor, losing interest, turns
To watch the brown slur of water,
Its gullies, gaps, adhesions, cancellations—
This is the firmament, however elusive.
This is the naturalism of the obscure.
Better to have names for the risen,
Call them word, visible, present.

NIGHT REHEARSAL

for Brighde Mullins

This is the ordeal of symmetry, persistent, staged.
Her hair on one side, thin wine on the other,
Some notion of burnished, of age,
Supporting the treasure now,
Even now, advanced.
Claw at the tide.
Parlay the answer into another saying
Or settle for the hard thing riding across the road
In wind. Night back, cold back, buttons burst,
Each of us lasting on the beautiful as is:
Mozart, Milton (*it is my habit night and day*
To seek for this idea of the beautiful, as for a certain
Image of supreme beauty) perched above us like a title,
And I alert to its position, as to a place for the heart,
Arguing for the referent in its full exposure
Who can never tell it all, not to him, not to you.

Whole weeks splurge like the history of cities,
Each house spawning another, each girl
Waiting. Her hair, burnished,
Falls across the black silk:
Carmen enhanced, or remembered, at the library.
So winter light ignites blue glass.
And so, as witness, I could see such pain
Mistaken for pleasure. The hard thing arrived
At its curb. The one who never knew never knew.
In this way we advanced, as the dead man
Came to write in the Sunday paper as if from the dead.
Immediacy is worse than prediction: it plays on.

No news from either coast.
The wild words obey their primary intelligence,

Forget their settings, forget their images,
Come riding across the road like hard things
Without hindrance, making a subtle new noise,
Marking an angle. Whole weeks splurge and,
In a small foreign city, a girl
Begins to know what nobody else ever knew,
Becomes accomplished despite her beauty.
I know, I know, she sings
Letting the boy take her to the ballet,
Letting her hair rush over black silk.
A cluster of fat starlings, ink blots, blooms,
Tinker on the nude branches, waiting it out.
Something is pushed, gently, from the tabernacle.
And over these pastures of plenty
Comes an audience of seekers who are not yet dismal.

TUSCAN VISIT (Simone Martini)

1.

Day leaned from its agency: a false, hollow gold,
An old temporary bridge, huge trees
Bunched over the night like night bunched
Into another language—

                        leaned, and sifted
Its warnings onto her.
It seemed to ask
Why carry these figures on your back
Why adhere when feet have already blossomed
On the slippery tile, and the carved faces
Look down, hidden and humorless because sacred.
That day was a little stung, a little ruined.
The girl had brought the weather with her
Like a toy blindly churning a smoky stench
Into the coiled trees. Yellow hedges,
Pruned into steps, where no one walked,
Where everyone had walked, were a riddle or task
Something in any case to enter willingly
As one passes into sight. The statues glared.
The bridge rattled like gunshot briefly, under pressure.
She thought of the voice she knew best and heard it arch
From side to side, stitching a canopy.
She could look nothing up.
She could only guess.

2.

It must have been early
Before light had split her unfinished skin of dream
And awakened the tumbling arc of saying—

                              In Siena, a sloped shell
                    Choreographed to wander to sleep to kiss
                    To run freely across to be sheltered
                    To eat to watch to talk—

Who is it?
It must have been early,
The ground newly splintered into grass,
Sitting on the porch, reading,
Sparrows stringing from limb to limb; early,
At dusk, swallows looping, long columns of gnats,
Bats pinching the air, dogs yapping in the courtyard,
The breeze breaching her ankles
Draped in the foreground, cool smoke
Lifting from the frame
A white scent
In which gold weather sat with gold birds
Depicting it
Who is it?

3.

A conspiracy of stars, night's umbilical blue
Shunt—details—shunt—
Looking at and being in
Have you seen my diary?
What time is it?
She twists away from her book—
What did she see?
The hills as a journey,
The sky as a sign,
Cypress beards—

It came as a subject
Lick, stamp, address
She twisted away
Shunt—details—shunt—
And stared
And startled
Disquiet, reflection, inquiry, submission, merit
Looking at and being in
A conspiracy of blues, night's umbilical star.

4.

Detained in such an arena, mute, subjected,
Consumed by what she could not know,
The trance of facts surrounding her,
Codes among the multitudes—
Would you save my place?
Flies, bees, birds
And the harbor full of boys
Sporting their nudity under other auspices,
Her love engraved like a platitude
On a charm, even her solitude—she

Hears the crest of bells
Through the patient door
Dividing her from it, it from us—
Inspired, installed, ceded.

5.

You go to a place, you stare
At the weather, naming it fondly.

You are amazed by the moon.
You say *portal* and *garment* to yourself
And notice the pressure of young fat thighs
Invested in satin. The trees
Ride in and out of the composition
And the hills, frescoed to the sky,
Are absorbed and absorbent in milky light.
You pluck stray flowers; you drink local wine.
You go to a place, you see
A woman trimmed in gold;
The women are trimmed in gold
And are not transparent.
You say to yourself *spine.*
You say *kneel, issue, wing*
As the map flies open into its depictions.
Her hand on the cowl of her robe,
Her small mouth turned down,
Her thumb holding a book open,
Her body recoiled from the offered lilies.

BOY SLEEPING

for Richard

These difficulties—flamboyant tide, modest red berries,
Or modest tide, flamboyant berries—
The moon keeping and casting light
Onto the boy's sleeping face
And the posture of his knowledge
Erected on the fatal—
                    Is this how it begins?
Or is the solid figure of the night
Only a wish to survive the last word said
So that such natural things induce furthering
After the episode of the shut.
Should I tell him his face mirrors the lost?
Should I tell him to wake, marry, find, escape

The one whose voice exhausts itself on the recurrent
Whose fraudulence speaks without images
Whose desire spends itself
On indifference, and whose light
Makes light of us, those of us whose bearing is
To continue—
                    What is the sublime
But a way, under the pressure of not knowing but caring,
To join the crowd at the slam, to lust openly
For the insecure moment when she turns, not yet dead,
And says: *I am coming with you nevertheless and because.*

I remember when a word
First advanced like a dart at a target,
A star creasing the sky, a lie
Told to save the situation while damning it.
I remember when the annual survey included nothing abstract

Because the war was full of particulars, particular events.
I remember a ride from the suburbs, sun setting in the windows,
Reminding me that I would forget, and so
Reminded me not to forget, although
The dead woman in the sleeping boy's face
Is a better example.
                                    How much we want to disobey
The sanctity of the kept,
To deny the already as it strides forward
Without introduction, revising
Before our eyes the unelicited partition of morning.
The precedent of the real mocks us.
Rain spills uncontrollably from above like a test.
Can we follow these new waters
Or are we already too fond, our agility mired
In the scripted river rushing under the bridge.
This is asked to keep us going one way or another
Lest the pause spread, flooding the field with reflection.
At the center of discourse, forgotten or unnoticed,
A train passes carrying a woman in her youth,
A terrorist, and a boy
Waking, wishing he were some place else.

III

THE ELABORATE
ABSENCE

HOW THINGS BEAR THEIR TELLING

for Joe Brainard

They settle out from their curfew
A splash of redemption, a ploy

Steeped in earliness
Listening is scenic

Uplifted ruffled boughs
Anchor the pond

To be near, tame and graphic
Small derivations drawn mutely forward

Footsteps on the pier
Quickly dry

His white cuffs open
His collar open

To fuse, conclude, adhere
To dangle and arrange

Along the road, a garden is waiting
Along the road, a house will be built

The painter's huge back—
The volume's tent

A celebration among strangers
A bride's opaque face

Where she travels she is
Harpoon in the back of a whale
. . .

Tinctures, sets, rips—
Leaping as conquest, as plot

A mower and an old man's booming voice
A chronology is mislaid

What is palpable is shunted—
The distance between landings

Deep in the foreground like a caress—
The breath draws in

There are these rims
These goggles clouded and abrupt

A narrative resembles a lost ornament
The dying resemble the living closely

Is someone really sawing the night?
Any choice is exclusive

Saying and crickets abide—
They forgot to put up signs

Both dice and sky are loaded—
The night is like Chicago

Seeing through to thought
A nude and voracious stranger

If you are stung, try cool air—
The sun is not a light bulb

. . .

Not so much spinning as raking
Not so much burning as fleeing toward

Days the size of postcards
Voyages along steps

Immediacy precludes reversal—
Jumping, he contained her pleasure

To touch, to refrain from touching
Nearness is its own, inexhaustible law

A temporal clerestory evades the threshold
No smears, no red ink

Stairs, halls, doors—
An incitement to hurt, to be inconclusive.

GESTURE AND FLIGHT

for Peter Straub

1.

She could be seen undressing
That is, in the original version
She could be seen undressing

A red jacket
Across a white chair

At first she had needed a coin,
A shelter, marriage, and these
Led quickly to her doubt

"feminine" "visceral"
Quoted rudely

Which then fell rudely
Through a ring and into her chamber
Where she could be seen undressing

A gesture, a glance
So the thing stood for its instance

Folded tidily under the lamplight
With the logic of fact.

In another instance, a volcano
Is hidden in the distance, a triangular hood
Under the sky's usual pan
And unusually adept clouds
But the image on the stamp is cloudless.
In yet another, masculine, version,

An arc intersects process
As ribbons of color are technically masked
So as not to bleed / her jacket
Falling off the chair as she turns, her mouth /
The gesture of the brush exploited, willfully exploited:
"volition" "deceit." And the girl's own story
Includes shoes, bottles, beds,
A jacket, hair

Then both or all sexes
Foregather under the island's moon
Without so much as an announcement from the captain
We are experiencing turbulence telling us
What we already know. Already lovers
Are rowing across the inlet
As the moon rises.
Let us hope there is no photograph of the event.

2.

A half-finished sensuality
Bloom, opiate
                    No
The partial locale of things
Residence, place
                    No
The ardor of the provinces
Well, how was Italy?
                    No

Spun from an initial prop—
Avoid the the—

So here goes this part—
Would into what looks like—
Family romance: caprice plus longing equals—
Vessel, accoutrement, waking—

Wake up!
Is the map a puzzle or the puzzle a map?
The sun is not an earring. The moon is not its mate.
Each variant shuffles into view or is shot
Through the hole where the button was
On colder mornings, and cloth
Is pinned to the wall with neon pilings.
Hardly a story yet and yet
Plot must be the succinct
Restored to its aftermath.
Turn her slowly, her here, ere he

Eerily, sun comes through as time, and I'm
Found in its provenance: trees and such and *plish,*
Wet polish over old boards where he and she stand
Among arresting branches, their countless
One and one and one. A picture? A map?
They must hear air moving among broken anomalies of air,
Its chant revived in the actuality of their needing it:
Hymnal, not critique, nothing to touch, to see, to eat.

That would be flight
But this, a ripped adventure
In tandem's everlasting grip, also
Is subject to song: so go on
Up the tune's horizon, up up up

Its prohibitive curl, snarl, smile
Almost as visible as

If only air could carry such inferences,
If things could be thusly sung,
An option of partial seeing
And of plentiful response

Each iteration—
Tentative plow, wild new damage—
Moving from stranger to stranger
Tracing, as if, an intimacy.

Ice doth hang stiffly.

3.

What were those kisses made of,
And those tissue-clad children,
Their remnants laid across the hills like fog?
Had she danced in the temple where the Egyptians lay?
Had they? That was the city's ruse
To keep us moving from station to station
Hoping for chance to erupt
From the dangerous crux of endings.
There is a list and everyone is on it.
But to be turned toward a discrete, ravelled flame
Composed of the foreground, lasting only as long as passage—
Could nearness ever suffice?
In this version, she takes a screen from its window
And air is relentless,

A rhythmic presentation of toward,
As the foggy grid subtracts to its object,
The object to its pile. Certainly,
She could be seen undressing
As she stretches her arms overhead
As she touches her shoe.

BLUE IRIS

1.

To notice only the harried span
Urgency twisting over urgency
As rain branches from the sky
And another, broken from its emblem,
Is a wound or flower
Briefly beyond what we can imagine
And so capture

I say these things after rain
After mist has leveled on the lake
Causing pictures to reside each night
Not exactly glad—and the artist's fatigue
With speaking her language, with listening,
Her lungs singed, sitting beside the dying boy
Who knows he is dying but does not say so
And the rain was like a company of strangers
Racing away from home

Everything now ample and wet
And the tall blue iris
Is the result of water
Unhurt where the sky could never be.

But is it ever enough to submerge
One question under another
And then to scramble for a vow
Bringing something—anything—to light?
In this instance, she
Is another young woman on a quest
For what she thinks should be but isn't

And the harm on the streets
Is another disappointment:
Poverty, and fear, and the drunk
Raging against his freedom to be drunk.
Nothing in nature is this estranged.
I had asked myself to stop and begin again
In a new quiet, to collapse on the meadow
And be obliging and commensurate, to play
In the quickening green
And not be afraid.
Things wave from their anchors.

2.

Wanting to include or to be included
Physical, natural, part of a habit she formed
Even as voices came from a certain distance
And the small, bright colors seemed solitary
Without another's approach, and the air
Laid down on the water
Its final reach,
Which could not be remembered.
Why not sit in a chair by the water's edge?
Why not see the sun hit glass?
There is always a precipice in the long twilight
Which is not chosen, lovely, dangerous, and inflected
By how it might be halted: not to go there would halt it
Or, being there, she might see nothing, hear nothing
And so not know she had been there.
Her dreams were full of scavengers.
Two long bodies fell from above
As the building swayed. Everyone else was calm.

She had many unexpected lovers.
It seemed everything came through an arch
To be presented, and stories unfurled in order to be told
And others not to be told although they, too, were included
In the mayhem of erasure. I heard the Chinese woman say
In English that no one had been killed
That the trucks had not run over
Only a few potted plants, a few old trees.
A few old trees are being moved slowly in the day's old air.

3.

The sun soothes each particular
Into a fluid settlement.
The lightness of the light is a passing option
And will be distilled by a later moon
Afloat for all to see.
Did the young artist feel better today?
Did the dying boy?
The bloom seems ardent because tall.
Blue has spilled into my mind
Like the blood that was not spilled
Over the picture of the dead face
And the quiet that surrounded her words.
She had said "trucks" with difficulty.
"The trucks, the trucks did not run over. . . ."

PROM IN TOLEDO NIGHT

La—la—la is the germ of sadness
said the speaker in sneakers
　　　　　—MICHAEL PALMER

A new heat comes up on a grand scale.
Were we waiting for it, as for a link,

Ask about sugar? Well, the heat is
Here. I thought I would speak of it

For someone to adjust the antenna, to

The recent suburban content, how much
Sky is now blocked. I have run into

Coolly, as flatly as possible, given

Chatted with both florists. Boys have
Been born to two nice women: Raphael

Numerous persons I know. I have

On a trial basis. I don't know why but
This heat is like a quarry dug into

And Penn. Some friends have separated

Omissions, intuitions flying out of the
Cranny or slot we thought irreducible,

The side of a hill. Intangible

Some things, uninteresting things,
Colors, pigs, toys, the usual river.
• • •

Earlier, I had written, mentioning

Radio: *I saw a good one, It looked like*
It could run. That was before the heat

I noted a couplet from a song on the

Cabaret. Another poem begins: "But
We were drawn away again by portraits,

But after I had won the howling dog at the

Those who were still living, but who
Had forgotten while the violins

Pictures where we could be idle against

I don't know what that means. The poem
Continues: "Beautiful faces

Explained the conditions

It seems someone else was in the room.
This is a Mercury Production.

Turn in the light; the two walk, stop

Evolving like the slow surge of history."
That part of the poem ends there, but

And then the spectacle
. . .

Room to its original strangeness, "I
Have better things to do with my time,"

Then another: "Restoring a

I mention it was prom night in Toledo?
Have you noticed how the specific is

Now that I am in the city again. Did

Continuities of what we want.
                              Of what

Always a gash or wound in the ongoing

Unravelled speaks for itself, a mask.
I'll stop concluding that desire is

We want to keep, to cure, care for. The

A girl rides from the field in hot sun.
We stopped, once, at a lake to swim

A good place to start. I'll quit, as

The old red Ford. Last night you said
My dreams would improve but

When the heat became intolerable in

And after April, when May follows,
And the whitethroat builds, and all the
. . .

You were wrong

On a black table, some around your house,
Some around mine, and the specific looms

Peonies weighted, three in a white vase

We turn and turn through always and ever
With as between us. When you laugh my

Again. In my mind there is a carousel,

The point of entry: the gash on the hill,
What we see as we ride. From the log:

Arms feel light. Your voice has become

A small Pa. town. Ducks, chickens, geese,
Fresh eggs. I had some bacon, too, I

2:15 your time. Stopped for lunch in

About that duplicated hill. As I write
Duplicated hill I look up and the first

Never eat bacon or eggs. I'm thinking

The sign says bridge may be icy. My
Mind revolves around where and when.

Big hill appears ahead. We walked East.
. . .

61

Trying to describe a miniature calla
Lily only makes matters worse, and

Passing Presque Isle

I grasp at particulars when I am a
Deposit of hermetic, avid cares

Proves your point about dimensions

Be, found in the radiant furl of skin
As it plummets, seen from under a

Whose known qualities could be, might

Akin. I can feel the city's nearness,
Its less than equal attitude in

Cluster of new foliage, or something

My bracelet got hitched to a girl's
Sleeve—a frenzy took place around

Skirmishes—elbows hit elbows, wrists

Is this a form of exaltation or despair?
I love conjecture, although its stipend,

Some running shoes on sale on the street

Linear vein pierced, is too delicate.
Interspersed among these less than valiant

Day after day of weather reports like a
. . .

My love, this is the bitterest, that
Thou / Who art all truth and who dost

Innings I'd turn to pure lyric:

Among the temporarily stricken; old
Litany of passage. Against a glass

Love me now . . . warble of language

I've come to see through nothing, ad-
Mit to only a haphazard verisimilitude

Backdrop and its brilliant flanges

Eyed art. Of course you, as both
Occasion and witness, pull me through

Similitude of the storyteller's wide

Gloss it amuses you to touch. I had
Planned to leave earlier, but these

Like a thread of feather whose pale

Suddenly the sense of prelude becomes
A hard spray of contingencies,

Keep making their mobile shadows

The most essential. She turns to look
Into the glass, watches as the image

. . .

63

Adamant, refuting, like a tax on

Of a gate closing off the garden for-
Ever. The model, exposed, could not

Expand, shifting to the calamity

With the rest, and nobody would know
How it ended, as nobody had known

Last, but would be shredded

Briefly wild; a fan eeked its rotations
Into an alley; her friend, a girl,

I have but to be with thee, and thy hand
She reads a line from the open page

Told her mildly, obliquely, to rescind

To increase or ease the new implication.
It was as if a lance, aimed into the night

Of a nearby volume, hoping for chance

Of a passing stranger who had been surprised
But had remained diffident as he plucked it out

Had hit a real target, had stung the arm

He had taken a rag, knotted it,
Walked uphill in the direction
. . .

And watched as blood poured from the hole

He had asked, handing her back the weapon
This tale boiled up from the flat black earth

From which the thing had come. *Is this yours?*

To breach the destitution of our aimless band's
Hungers. The more familiar pattern

One long spring whose sole aim appeared to be

Became interesting only when we decided
To participate in it. The room

This habit of one thing leading to another

Airless so that she, in it, felt
Breathless, reckless, faithless

Painted a virulent green, seemed

As I sleep, an unnatural extremity prevails.
I am entrusted to a stranger, harnessed

I have but to be with thee, and thy hand

A spill I try to prevent like this.
Did you use a cup for the dice?

Or yoked while floodgates are lifted
· · ·

With either the actual or absolute.
In the full heroic flush, we

Am I *A?* Each line is a quibble

How can I keep an even keel: "Single tree
In brown field: two trees: flashing

Could not be more discerning, note

Empty corrals: white fences: cows:
Arrows: your fingers: your: small bird

On barns: silver: wrists: your fingers:

Like a beacon: the smell of oats:
Right lane ends; Merge left: you

Attacking hawk: shade: that green silo

Different hair: your . . ."
                              Being marked

By the river, those girls with

Solitude cheats, it is to you I am speaking
While at the same time wanting a world

As thought: what to suggest, what elicit?

Of how it looks but how it is. You
Are the constituent object; this distance

Others might recognize, not because
• • •

                    Others will say
She was just passing the time—

An argument. Against what?

Animal allegiance—makes dinner from scratch
Abating or diluting while the last thrash—

A milder form of discourse

The river is nearer. Little conversations
At the checkout counter.

Still to be seen against—I am less at ease—

I remember the room I invented you in,
How happily captive I felt in such

At last, a reductive mood

Exactitude in this, an idea of being
As being with. This is rudimentary

Confinement. There was, and is

Say love is an attitude toward difference
In its freest form, adhering, inimical

But festive, if the subject persists

Now, let's leave to the cartographers
While the music lasts, the privileged
    • • •

To time's jurisdiction. Space for

Most intimate, most entailing.
Abundance and loss are the terms.

Information a display, a harbor

The arch or bridge or catapult—
A dart piercing an arm—is how

Earn the right to ford the rapids.
That she wants to converse in silence

We redress, reconceive our predicament

The unutterable collapse of particulars
Yet speaks its priority and stillness.

Is how desire crumbles disbelief

Men skip succinctly over the drawbridge
Muscular and vibrant in the distilled age

Pleasure is the cost of time, as may be

Some future proverb in which complexity is
Soothed: give the infant beer for her tooth.

The women darken with expertise, hum

Blooming above the pond in memory. Our task
Is to be less defeated by these children
. . .

But the fireworks were only partly successful

Girl is out of control, she reaps her hunger
On small things, rips handfuls of blooms,

As they shrilly discard the air. The golden

Seeing what I contain, as one contains
An ancient song. *La La La,* a spray of notes

Rips hair, my only sight, now actually

Stick to cloth, home sweet home as awful
As a flood, a crowd, an epidemic beyond halt.

In heat, an absent, singular source. Words

Cure for the incommensurate. *La La:* who cares
In the fresh air to which we now, even now,

Rapture is the antidote, as may be.

NOT THAT IT COULD BE FINISHED

She holds a conversation with her ornaments,
Stray or contingent, heaped in patches
Darkly and then loosened
Onto the table to be consumed.
Collect me, they seem to ask,
Into an assembly; construe us
Like any morning onto any day.
Bring us forward notch by notch
Into a paradigm of comfort
To be clasped: any cup will do.
Any dance? Take a seed
And blow it toward the curtain
Which, like a bright shield
Hugging breasts into radiance,
Is seen and spoken of and desired.
Will any silence fit? So many
Columns of air are held upright
In inebriated passage,
So many paper stacks
Brittle under the weight
Of what was news to attentive readers
As zones of holy strangers
Feed through tunnels their imported cares.
Stare at us, they seem to say,
We are windows propped up against the sky,
Quotations of light waiting to sail
Into your aperture, calling *because because*
And *now now now*. And the good body
Is pulled over the original rapacious body
Like a huge sock, its cornucopia
Of sour wind and dust emptied into the firmament.

NOTES FROM A CONVERSATION

for Kit White

A shuffle loaded its merits brightly
As we reached to touch them
And to name their parts.
In the neighborhood of illusion, stripped
Of its wholeness and so longing to be whole.
The jury was sequestered as usual,
A dream locked in sleep, from which the day
Would open upon explanation, unaided and alert.
What remained of yesterday's choices?
A claim check, tokens, a boy
With wet feet and a sheaf of papers.
"That Tuesday it rained."

In the new dispensation, conspiracy
Will be replaced by
Collusion, the diction of the age
Filtered through the great sieve of particulars
To be sorted out later, as in the bald
Absenteeism of June,
Pebbles forgotten or supposed,
Link relinquishing link
In a quarrel over obedience,
Its own refusal to arrive
On the watery thrust, or to shine
In a voice once recognized
The whose of it laid out in common noise
So as not to observe the body's subject
Just ended. The woman was pretty
And spoke cogently, despite
The thin hose up her nostril.
It rained that Tuesday, and the news

Picked up from where the fiction had left off.
Was this a brave epistemology?
By midmorning, the sun had ironed
Every wrinkle and erased both puddle and footprint.

BROKEN SKYLIGHT

for Brian Conley

Adjusting the radar to desertion   less heat needed
More sure than certain   fewer feet away than
The list grows pursuant to the is-factor
Where *f* finds find but *a* alas, also
A self as a vacancy with language schemes
                                        This example
Proportional exhibit and banished weather
The one in doodle clothes
Waiting to know something large
Enough to measure, get to, and escape.
The same *if* presents itself
As conclusively abandoned
Sounds like shores
But is music after all, temper or bridge
Talismanic, virtual, or stilled
                                        & another thing
Could come as an explosion out of thin air
Ripple of screen, conversation at lunch
Fires running on into the night
& looked away from as a child might

In the parade's deft narration
Anyone could join the party

Fun is dialectical but who rules the roles
& to give the little guy stature
Rained out among the multitudes
Margins to be occupied
The donkey's tail in the eye

To loop through the marble's insignia
They contained passage, the heat's starvation

Taken to its limit, attraction
Forbidden in the upsurge,
Glory contaminated by the personal,
With optional wit.
The old neighborhood is embedded in event,
The calamity of event.
One drawing indicates another room
As if to bring drama to the surface
One talent barking after another in the skit
Before the longed-for intermission.
Go out into the clinking evening's
Unfettered air, the elegant morass.
Young persons are wrapped so tightly
They seem to miss it
As it wanders over the horizon's sentence.
Nothing supersedes the applicable
But the blessing, delirium's old exchange.

Behaving as usual had its portents.
In certain repetitions, an obvious and started rupture.
Nothing's plenitude.
A sojourn whose excellence drained itself as climate.
We, among others, could discuss how to pronounce it.
Every perfection is harmful if swallowed.
Things fade evenly enough, given plenitude.
I look across the ocean and see more ocean.
So much is strange in the environment.
The film of course is fiction.
What comes up comes up.
Don't forget to water the anemones.

OPENING DAY

for Charles Bernstein

Locally a firm disavowal within the drift.
Shaman of discourse said
Or could have said
These logics go teasingly forward
Into capacities, and then the then.
Ifs warrant their source, their excuse,
Since the palliative OK
Is already subsumed in reaction:
All this enlarging the vestibule's
Urban decay to which we happily assent
As it makes our news worthy.
Fine judges the finite in characteristic measures,
Retained or not, but bet on the illiterate
In their Bible mode and the market for new voices.
Transparent underclass of the forgiven-forgotten
And the big otherness
Freed up on this mountainous hell
Where cusp meets cusp between buzzards.
In age, the mouth betrays its detractors,
Mood swings swing unexpectedly toward what was.
Subjects are a catastrophe for the simplest will.

From the perspective of the will, goaded, crested,
Inviolate third party
Beams toward a new era via
Uncertain coalitions of—what?—souls
Nearing sound and underwritten
By an autobiographical thumbnail sketch
At the Indian restaurant.
Said *dead* on occasion. Said it again
Made numerous as if grown at marginal speed
So shreds assembled their interim hope

Whose attachment might be
Ask me how to live.
Weather's avalanche from street to street
The garden surrounded by flying debris
Men in their soft linen masks. She
Can't get you out of her dreams
Her student suggests she sell her body
She might have been an astronomer had she
Noticed that gap, that emblem of

An arcane receptacle for borrowing
And for being heartened
By the absence of a prefix
And so lodged in a more definite surround.
Breathing entities, gladly present,
Send good wishes as fights for life
Under the headlined insurgency
Whisper on the other side of the curtain
In the public area, now international as any
Idle promise. If what is missed
Is the agency and its shelter
What is gained is action
Whose siren gathers all to it
As to the late, lamented flame.
Save what? When?
Take a picture of the moment
And send it home to where things are told
At far below market value all the year long.

Cauldron preserved as sun-dried apricots
Freewheeling and soon to be told
If not tasted, praising the then

Already mentioned as a design's design.
Periodicity unfurls, messing up the evening
And the food is discerned as raving mad
Insofar as the *prix* is fixed.
All this tea, these chimes
Cavorting as shapes whose frequency is chosen
Even as one people's icons are assimilated
Into the mall with the purpose of a trend.
Small vicissitudes are fretted uneasily into music
To which all come but few can hear.
A blockade of sorts, and a wager
While the moon's coinlike appearance
Confirms the darkness
And the swift corseting of lovers
Discarding their targeted desires.
Some games are classic, move by move.

Whereas babble became in time defunct
And retreat made history
Improbable if not assuaged
The dark bloom
Previously unnoted
Holds more than testimony
And gender's alternative issue.
The big fish ate the tiny fish and grew bigger.
The upside-down mask smiled.
Unburdened knowledge is offensive
Given the sports motif. To acquire
Is to be accountable, but who is counting
When stars insist on their same contingency.
The clearing's gesture would come later.
It would not solve the pious nor rectify its spin.

Affinity has its fevers: gold
Amphitheater of the mind,
Indignity of the wept.
I watched him walk into the meadow
The wind, well, you know, windylike.
I don't know exactly.
Tag line: spirit, winterkill, mortgage, prize.

THE ELABORATE ABSENCE

for Mei-Mei Berssenbrugge and Richard Tuttle

1.

To think   invisible   is therefore
                    partition/parturition
                            parturiunt montes (nascetur ridiculus mus)
        not to be
pronounced/selfsame ludicrous pallor/forgetful nude
ascending.
Cascade beauty   aspect/guise of the lucid
    nomenclature of light said light said
    dropped one location/found another
                                    as love
        over and missing its
                    hearing
        not encountering/room
        for sorrow's construal in age in adage.
Anyway the harmonies as she looked up into the listening
    speaking in her attire/entire
    volition of the spoken to
    in among the
    room full of   (white on white walls)
                                    & acquainted with.
Plenitude of stark persuasion/lost footing
                    excellent motif could eat could ingest
Mirth of angels after a catastrophe/name ten
Let it fend for itself/watch TV   be consoled   if it were
Then why not buy a mesa sit atop build a replica
Flooded with or by
                        unanswerable gold.

2.

Then some weed/urban episodic gall
Punctilious venom
          excess
Parade of familiars
You name it/what color to paint the trim
See-through stitches
What great weed enamored of its poison
And the after-effects of Eden's bipartisan namings.

Neither to compete nor to restrain
Tether of the taught
But in the room/New Yorked
Like a flame of/or better yet ticker-tape parade
With party favors, miniature cartoons, girl
Bare-breasted crooning her tunes in the cathedral blimp.
I have a famous unease. You
Are as well as can be expected. We
Must attend the anniversary dinner of the undisclosed.

3.

Season stalled/intractible basket/yolk
Smeared in the rotted web/accrual of whispers
Looming in fog: *please do not knit*: girl
In first weather of girlhood
Held up over the world
                    to see. And behind
Folds in the veil, beyond
Tearing open the envelope/blank
Blanket & saying its private parts/in the tub

I wash my heart. Acrid sting of befouled waters.
Dirt of the unsurpassed/to be mended or emptied out.

4.

Whose hands? In whose hands?
An assembly standing on the ice pit and an owl
Taking the troupe on into the woods, to Madrid,
Paris, Berlin: come along, children, *kinder, mes enfants*
Leave her to melt in the spring sun
Over the broken spillway. Her bones will freeze/white
On white walls. And this chamber
Is an inversion of that one, see?
Not a reflection, but an upside-down equation: now
You are walking on the ceiling
Now you are making your way through a plastic forest
With slits/if you see light look through it/her body
Cast/flowering/ long white scars
Invisible/untold.
                    Whose hands
Said you cannot enter the world with an idea of the
    world/ticket
Torn at the edge/entrance
Into the mesh/exit
Onto the risen plantation.

5.

Riddle scooped out/tender bell
Machine is on leave word
A basket of
                    at the door.

To not to

Erase/truckloads of ciphers/urgent prize
And response/promises foretold as if weather.

6.

Riddle of re-

    an attempt to decipher its mate
    the age of any ordinary day
    arranged as sound
    wanting the throng to return/one kiss
    begets another & look over his shoulder for proof
    ancient fist of notes

Riddle of re/wrapped in plain linen placed in a box
Father in ashes/wrap me.

7.

Girl stands in front of a window in a long white dress.
Behind the window the moon is full, shining its light
In on the young girl in the white dress.
Young girl's brother is standing by a piano.
He looks at his sister, the young girl
Looking like a painting of a young girl in moonlight.
Speak, he says to his sister, *speak. Say dog.*

8.

Thirst excelled   monumental   disowned
Parched reveries: to see not to want, to want, not to care
                    modulated parts/flee

Studded with cans
    hanging
Stars in their gangs/some

                                     solace, the compass
Excited by refrains
Palpable weather introduced as curiosity/strapped down
To eternity as the background frays

                                  and what festivity
Waits, what bird whose shrill
Damages space.

9.

Between the aesthetic and confrontation/trades
Let us divorce/be equipped to/imperfect, restive
To grips with/allow and bring your color swatches/galoshes
Feel free to help yourself
Under the rotunda of autumn, incision
Struck dumb in ornamental outcropping
By what measure is hell cast/black stones/rocks/ moss
And so jocular and evasive in analysis/open the cloud
Radar of angels in the spooky village of childhood
Say dog fraught with pages   loyal incendiary
Shoulders culled into colors above the podium aloud
Settle down in the grotto to watch/master of tirades/tryst
Affinity/ontology of the guide/leaves where they may

10.

Stare into the lagoon of the beloved, open
Another file, abjure

                        sometimes, after all, emptied.

My girl,
Be not furtive even as the truck is lessened of its burden
And the floor, again, is clean.
The lake is aflame.
And lest you, of all, forget,
Keep it in mind with or without its target, its tune.